JoJo & Bow Bow

RAZZLE-DAZZLE BABYSITTERS

BY JoJo SIWA

nickelodeon

AMULET BOOKS
NEW YORK

Cataloging-in-Publication Data has been applied for and may be obtained from the Library of Congress.

ISBN 978-1-4197-4596-6

ABRAMS The Art of Books
195 Broadway, New York, NY 10007
abramsbooks.com

CONTENTS

CHAPTER 1

"I'm still not sure why you set up this emergency get-together at Maria's Pizza," JoJo said, smiling at her best friend, Miley, as she helped herself to a slice of pepperoni pizza, "but I definitely approve of the location!"

JoJo sighed happily as she inhaled the delicious aroma of fresh-from-the-oven pizza. She could tell by the steam coming off her slice that it was still too hot to taste. She took another look at Miley. "I also approve of that new hairstyle you've got going on," JoJo added. Miley had the top section of her long, wavy dark hair pulled into a messy bun with a velvet scrunchie, leaving the bottom part cascading around her shoulders.

"Aww, thanks! You always notice when something is even a teeny bit different," Miley commented.

"As your BFF, it's my job to notice these things," JoJo joked. "Seriously, though, Miley, what's up? Everything okay?"

Miley nodded as she fanned a hand over her own slice, trying to cool it off. "Everything is fine! I just felt like I needed a little break. With homework, choreography stuff, visiting Dusty, and ice-skating lessons, it seemed like I hadn't seen you in forever! Then I remembered that we had yet to try this place, which is supposed to be the best new spot in town, and thought a pizza date sounded like the perfect idea!"

"Pizza dates are always a perfect idea!" JoJo agreed. "And good for you for knowing when to say you need a break." JoJo paused and lowered her voice. "Although . . . not that I'm complaining . . . but we did just see each other over the weekend!"

"Really?" Miley burst into giggles. "Well it *felt* like forever!"

"Did you girls try the pizza yet?" Mrs. McKenna asked from the neighboring table. "It lives up to the hype!" Miley's mom often let the girls sit together at their own table in restaurants while she sat nearby and caught up on work emails. They would not have minded one bit if she sat with them, of course, but both JoJo and Miley appreciated the private time together.

"I've waited long enough. I'm going in!" JoJo announced. She carefully folded her slice, raised it to her mouth, and took a big bite. A slow smile spread over her face. "Oh em gee, this might be the best pizza *ever*. It's got the perfect cheese-to-sauce ratio, and the crust is . . ." JoJo opened her eyes and realized Miley wasn't even paying attention! She was twisted around in her seat, looking toward the front of the restaurant.

"Don't look now, but I'm pretty sure Goldie Chic just walked in!" Miley whispered.

"Really?" JoJo tried to look casual as she leaned out of the booth to scope things out.

"I think you're right," she said a moment later. The famous designer had such a unique look that JoJo doubted it could be anyone other than her. From her signature long brown hair to her gold bangles to her glittery cat-eye glasses, the tall woman at the front of the restaurant looked *exactly* like Goldie Chic.

"She has a little girl with her. Is that her daughter?" JoJo knew a lot about Goldie because her friend Kyra was a huge fan of hers, but she couldn't remember if the designer had a daughter.

"I think so. I can't *believe* Kyra's not here with us," Miley cried, as if reading JoJo's mind. "Maybe we can ask her for an autograph for Kyra after she sits down. What do you think?"

JoJo thought about it. As someone who was often asked for her autograph, she knew how great it felt to meet and connect with a fan. On the other hand, maybe Goldie just wanted to have a quiet dinner with her daughter.

But JoJo didn't have to decide because a moment later Goldie Chic and her daughter stopped by *their* table!

"I'm so sorry to interrupt your meal,"

Goldie said smoothly, a friendly smile lighting up her face. "But my niece back in New York is a huge fan of yours, JoJo! Can I get your autograph for her?"

"Of course!" JoJo exclaimed. She scooted over in her seat in the booth. "Would you like to sit down for a minute?"

Goldie looked over at Mrs. McKenna, who nodded and smiled, and then gracefully slid into the booth.

"This is my best friend Miley"—JoJo gestured to Miley as she introduced her—"and that's her mom, Mrs. McKenna, in the next booth."

"It's so nice to meet all of you!" Goldie exclaimed. "And this"—she bounced the little girl on her lap—"is Lacey."

"Hi!" Lacey exclaimed, waving to everyone.

"Hi, there," JoJo said, waving back. "It's nice to meet you!"

Lacey grinned and then buried her head in her mother's ruffled blouse.

"Are you feeling a little shy?" JoJo asked. Lacey peeked her head out, giggled, and then buried her head again.

"So we saw you come in and were going to ask for *your* autograph for our friend Kyra," Miley explained as JoJo fished a pad of paper out of her pink-striped backpack. "We were just discussing whether it would be okay to say hi when you walked over!"

"I always love meeting fans," Goldie replied graciously. "But I appreciate that you were so thoughtful about it. Unlike me, just barging over here and interrupting your meal! But my niece would probably disown me if she ever found out I was in the same place as JoJo Siwa and didn't get an autograph!"

JoJo grinned. "What's your niece's name?"

7

"Vienna," Goldie replied. "Can I have a sheet of paper to autograph for your friend? Her name's Kyra?"

"Yep, Kyra." Miley nodded. "She's a designer too, and a huge fan of yours! She was telling me how you started designing when you were about our age . . ."

JoJo snuck a smile at Miley as she wrote a message to Vienna. Miley was a pretty big fan of Goldie's too, but she was using her time with Goldie to talk up Kyra. Reason number 4, 237 why Miley was such an amazing friend!

JoJo finished with the autograph for Vienna and slid it, an extra piece of paper, and the pen over to Goldie.

"We draw now?" Lacey asked, her eyes lighting up as she watched the exchange.

"Not now, sweetheart," Goldie said. But Lacey had already wrapped her little fingers around the pen.

"I have plenty of paper . . . ," JoJo said quietly so Lacey couldn't hear her. "And a bunch of colored pencils in my bag. Just sayin' . . ."

"Oh, okay!" Goldie laughed as Lacey clutched the pen in her fist like it was a treasure she would never let go of.

"Can I trade you that one pen for all these colored pencils?" JoJo asked Lacey.

Lacey's eyes widened when she saw the handful of brightly colored pencils JoJo was offering. She promptly dropped the pen. JoJo retrieved it and then spread out the pencils on the table in front of Lacey so she could begin drawing.

"And here is the autograph for Kyra," Goldie said a few moments later after writing a message to Kyra and signing her name with flourish.

"I love your bag," JoJo exclaimed to Goldie as she tucked the autograph in the front pocket of her own backpack. "Miley, it kind of reminds me of that scarf Kyra designed . . ."

"Absolutely!" Miley agreed.

"So Kyra designs scarves?" Goldie asked. "Is she only into accessories, or clothes too?"

"She does it all," Miley said. As Miley explained some of Kyra's work, JoJo pulled her phone out of her bag. She scrolled through the photos to look for the shots of her and her friends wearing the outfits Kyra had designed for Miley's birthday party.

"Here are some pics of ice-skating cos-tumes she designed," JoJo said, trying to hand her phone to Goldie.

"Play games!" Lacey cried, reaching for JoJo's phone.

"Oh no, sweetie, that's JoJo's phone," Goldie said, gently prying Lacey's fingers away from the phone. "She just wants to show Mommy something."

10

Lacey's face scrunched up.

"Will you do something for me?" JoJo asked, sliding the phone over to Miley so it would be out of Lacey's line of sight.

Lacey frowned, and her lip trembled a bit. JoJo knew that toddlers had a hard time with being told "no," and she had just a few moments to distract her before she possibly melted down.

"Will you draw me a picture?" JoJo continued. "Just for me, and I can keep it forever?"

"Of what?" Lacey asked.

"Hmmm . . . how about a pizza? With sprinkles and ice cream on top?"

Lacey clapped her hands and started drawing.

"You're so good with her," Goldie exclaimed as she accepted the phone from Miley under the table. "It's a shame you're not a little older—I'd hit you up for babysitting!"

"Aw, thanks," JoJo replied. "I love little kids."

Goldie nodded as she scrolled through the photos. "Wow, she's really talented," she said a minute later. "I'm loving that glitter edging she did. That's a really hard detail to do . . ." She looked more closely at one of the photos. "But that bomber jacket she made for your guy friend? That's the bomb dot com!"

"Right?" JoJo and Miley exclaimed at the same time.

Goldie smiled and handed the phone back to JoJo. "Your friend has a lot of talent. Please tell her I said so!"

"I wish she was here so you could tell her in person," Miley replied.

"We will make sure to bring Kyra with us on all future pizza outings, just in case we ever run in to you again," JoJo joked.

"Sounds like a plan." Goldie laughed. "Though going out tonight was a rare treat for me. I'm in the middle of launching my new collection and have been working non-stop. And I need to find a babysitter for Lacey. We just moved here from New York, and I don't have one yet." Hearing her name, Lacey looked up from the picture she was drawing to smile at everyone and then went back to drawing. "Do you girls happen to have any friends who are a little older and into babysitting by any chance?"

"It's too bad you need someone older," JoJo responded. "Kyra is practically a pro with kids!"

"I have a suggestion," Mrs. McKenna said, leaning over from the neighboring booth. "When Miley was little, the girl who lived next door used to do some supervised babysitting for me. She'd come over and play with Miley while I was home so there was still an adult present, but it was enough of a relief for me that I could get stuff done. And Miley loved it because she got to hang out with an older girl."

"That could work . . . ," Goldie said, nodding her head. " And is Kyra as good with kids as you are, JoJo?"

JoJo grinned. "She *loves* kids! She's done some supervised babysitting for our friend Jacob's little brother. I have to check with her, but I'm sure she'll be on board!"

"Great, let's make it happen!" Goldie said.

Lacey looked up from her drawing and grinned. "Let's make it happen!" she repeated.

"I think we're going to have our hands full with this little cutie!" JoJo laughed.

CHAPTER 2

"**M**om, I can't believe you have Goldie Chic's phone number in your phone!" Miley exclaimed as she and JoJo climbed into the backseat of Mrs. McKenna's car after dinner.

"We only exchanged numbers so I can put her in touch with JoJo's mom to talk about the babysitting." Mrs. McKenna chuckled.

"Thanks again for doing that," JoJo said as she settled in and fastened her seat belt.

"No problem." Mrs. McKenna smiled at the girls in the rearview mirror as she drove through the parking lot. "And you know what I can't believe? That you girls polished off almost an entire pizza on your own!"

"I might have had one slice too many," JoJo admitted as she clutched her stomach. "But it was sooooo good!"

"We should order takeout from there for our sleepover Friday night," Miley said.

"Thinking about more pizza already?" JoJo teased. "THAT is why we're best friends!"

For the rest of the ride home, JoJo and Miley talked about how incredibly nice Goldie Chic was, how utterly adorable Lacey was, and how over-the-moon excited Kyra was going to be when she found out she had the opportunity to meet her idol and help babysit her daughter. Miley didn't think she was going to be able to join them because her schedule was so packed with other obligations. JoJo understood and was proud of her BFF for not overbooking herself. JoJo knew better than anyone how easy it was to try to do too much!

Miley and JoJo made a pact not to tell Kyra until they were all together. Luckily they wouldn't have to wait very long, because they all had plans to hang out at their friend Grace's house after school the next day!

"You know we're at Georgie's house, don't you, BowBow?" JoJo laughed as her adorable teacup Yorkie barked excitedly as they approached Grace's front door. BowBow was doggie besties with Grace's corgi puppy. Seeing the two pups play together was one of the cutest sights in the world, if you asked JoJo.

BowBow yipped again as JoJo knocked on the door.

"We can't just barge in," JoJo patiently explained. "We have to be polite and wait for them to answer the door!"

Just then the door swung open, and JoJo was greeted by Grace's smiling face. "Were you just explaining manners to BowBow?" Grace laughed as she gave JoJo a welcoming hug.

"Someone has to," JoJo quipped as she followed Grace inside. She deposited Bow-Bow on the ground, and she immediately scampered off to greet Georgie, who started dancing around the moment she spotted BowBow.

"Everyone's already here," Grace said as she motioned for JoJo to follow her into the kitchen.

JoJo greeted her friends, feeling the usual shiver of happiness that always struck her when she saw them. JoJo knew she had an amazing group of friends: Grace, a talented artist who was as kind and sweet as she was loyal; Kyra, who was not only a fantastic designer but also a strong, fierce girl who always stood up for her friends; Jacob, a super skilled baker who was also hilarious and one of JoJo's oldest friends; and of course Miley, who was . . . well, Miley was just the perfect friend in about a million ways!

Because she was homeschooled, JoJo didn't get to spend the day with her friends, which was hard sometimes because she wondered about the fun times she was missing out on. But she and her friends always made time in their very busy schedules for after-school get-togethers like this one. Catching up with her friends was one of JoJo's favorite ways to relax and unwind.

"So how was your day?" Jacob asked as JoJo settled onto a tall stool at the kitchen counter.

"I think it just got about a million times better," JoJo said as she pointed to a plate of mini cupcakes. "Did you make those?"

"Sure did." Jacob grinned. "I'm trying out new flavors, so I made minis. I actually need you guys to be official taste testers for me. My aunt asked me to make cupcakes for her friend's bridal shower. She wants something involving raspberries, so I came up with three options."

"Well, the raspberry and chocolate gets my vote," Kyra said, licking icing off her fingers. "That one was redonkulously delicious!"

"I don't know, the raspberry vanilla crème was basically out of this world," Miley said.

"Sorry to make this even more complicated, but I vote for the raspberry peanut butter," Grace said a moment later.

Jacob turned to JoJo. "It's up to you! You have the tie-breaking vote!"

"Too much pressure!" JoJo sighed. "Ugh, the things I do for my friends . . ."

JoJo piled one of each of the mini cupcakes onto a plate. First she took a bite of the chocolate raspberry. It was perfection. Then she tasted the vanilla raspberry. It too was perfection. *Uh oh,* JoJo thought. *Please let the peanut butter raspberry be awful to make this a little easier.* But it wasn't awful. It was absolutely, positively scrumptious.

"Jacob, I don't know if I can pick one!" JoJo cried.

"But you have to!" Jacob pleaded. "Just tell me the first one that pops into your head when I ask you which one tasted best. Ready? Which one tasted best?"

"Raspberry peanut butter!" JoJo blurted out.

Kyra and Miley groaned as Grace cheered. "Wow, that was easy!" JoJo said. "I like that trick!"

With that business out of the way, the friends continued to catch up. Miley and JoJo were waiting for the right moment to tell Kyra their good news about Goldie Chic. They listened as Grace talked about an upcoming book report for school that she was nervous about.

"I've already read the book, and I know I can write a good report, but the part I'm nervous about is standing up in front of the whole class," Grace explained, gently tugging on the end of her long red side braid.

JoJo nodded sympathetically. Public speaking came easily to her because she was used to performing, but Grace was shy, and JoJo could imagine how giving a book report in front of her whole class could be a little scary.

"Well, the best thing you can do is practice, practice, practice!" JoJo said.

"In front of who? Georgie?" Grace joked.

"In front of us, silly!" JoJo replied. Her friends all nodded.

"You guys are as busy as I am," Grace said, picking at the cupcake wrapper on her plate. "And I need a LOT of practice. I can't ask you to sit around listening to me give my book report over and over again . . ."

"You can practice a bunch of times in front of a mirror," Miley suggested. "Just to get comfortable doing it."

"That's a great idea." JoJo nodded. "And you should video yourself too, and then watch it back. Trust me when I tell you it's always good to practice in front of a camera before going live!"

"Those are all good suggestions," Grace said. JoJo could tell she was relaxing a bit.

"And you can practice with me as many times as you want until you're ready for a bigger audience," Kyra said, putting an arm around her best friend. "We can practice on each other since I'm in your class and will have to give a report too!"

"But you're not terrified of public speaking!" Grace replied.

"Well . . . I can be . . . shy sometimes . . . ," Kyra began. But she couldn't keep a straight face, and neither could anyone else. One thing Kyra was not was shy.

"Thanks for trying to make me feel better," Grace said finally. "And I'll definitely take you up on your offer, Kyra. We can work together!"

"It's a deal!" Kyra agreed.

"Speaking of deals . . . ," JoJo began, making eye contact with Miley. "So, Kyra, Miley and I kind of have a deal for you . . ."

JoJo and Miley took turns telling their friends about their chance meeting with Goldie Chic. After many, many interruptions from Kyra, who was squealing so much that

BowBow and Georgie came running into the kitchen, ears raised at high alert, JoJo finally got to the part where Goldie wanted to meet Kyra and was trying to arrange to have the girls babysit for her.

"Well? What do you think?" JoJo asked. Kyra had gone from squealing in delight to complete and utter silence.

"I think I'm going to faint," Kyra said.

"Here, have some sugar," Jacob joked, putting a cupcake on her plate.

"My mom is going to call your mom to talk through all the details," JoJo explained. "Goldie already called my mom. The only thing is, Goldie wanted to know if we could do it on Friday night and—"

"Yes, of course we can do it on Friday night!" Kyra exclaimed.

"—And I was about to say, we have our sleepover planned for that night, remember?

So I was saying maybe we can find a night the following week—"

"JoJo, we can't tell Goldie Chic to wait until next week!" Kyra cried. She turned to face her friends. "Is there any way we can reschedule our sleepover for Saturday night? Pretty please with glitter and rainbows on top?"

Miley bit her lip, pretending to be deep in thought. She exchanged a wink with Grace and Jacob.

"Just glitter and rainbows?" Miley asked. "Throw in some unicorns and you've got a deal!"

Kyra jumped up and pulled her friends into a big group hug. "I have the best friends in the whole world!"

CHAPTER 3

"I love this outfit you decided on," JoJo said to Kyra as she slid into the backseat of Mr. Gregory's car. It was Friday evening, and Kyra's dad was driving them to Goldie Chic's house for their babysitting job.

"I thought the leopard scarf popped the most against this color." Kyra gestured to her lilac sweatshirt and continued, "Plus the purple matches my streaks. So you think I made the right choice?"

"Your outfit is on point, just like the other seven outfits you texted me pictures of!" JoJo laughed. She hadn't seen Kyra this nervous since . . . well, since EVER. JoJo hadn't known that calm, cool, and collected Kyra could even *get* nervous. But she understood that meeting your fashion idol was nerve-wracking when you were a designer yourself—even if you were super confident like Kyra usually was.

"You know she's going to love you, right?" JoJo reached across the seat to squeeze Kyra's hand in a reassuring way. "I mean, she's super nice, she already thinks you're talented, and you have a ton in common with each other. Just relax and be yourself!"

"That sounds like the kind of advice you give the Siwanatorz," Kyra said with a grin. "Which is fitting, since I am one!"

"True, I do say that the best way to deal with bullies is to just be yourself and not worry about what others think," JoJo said earnestly. "But the advice works now too, even though Goldie Chic is definitely *not* a bully! Just be yourself and you'll do great!"

"Sounds like wonderful advice to me," Mr. Gregory said from the front seat.

"Thanks, Mr. G!" JoJo replied.

"And on that note . . ." Mr. Gregory slowed to a stop at the end of a long driveway. "We're here!"

JoJo and Kyra said a quick goodbye to Mr. Gregory and ran to the front door. Goldie and Lacey must have heard them pull up, because the door swung open before they could even knock.

"Hi, girls!" Goldie exclaimed, extending her arm to welcome JoJo and Kyra inside.

JoJo looked around the spacious foyer. From what she could see so far, Goldie's flawless design sense applied to her home décor as well! The entrance hall was bright and airy, with gleaming white wood floors and the coolest metallic braided rugs JoJo had ever seen.

"Someone has been very excited about your arrival," Goldie said, gesturing to Lacey, who was hiding behind her mom's legs and giggling.

JoJo knelt down to greet Lacey as Goldie ushered Kyra into the living room. JoJo heard Goldie compliment Kyra's scarf just as Kyra complimented Goldie's earrings, and then the two of them broke into easy laughter.

"It's such a thrill to meet you," Kyra was saying, her voice strong and confident. "I think JoJo and Miley already told you, but I am a *huge* fan!"

JoJo grinned as she scooped Lacey up. Kyra didn't sound nervous at all! JoJo was proud of her friend for finding her natural confidence and putting it on display. She waited a moment for them to get to know each other a bit and then decided it was time for Kyra to finally meet Lacey. She walked over to where Goldie and Kyra were and gently plopped Lacey down.

"So, Kyra, this little superstar is . . ."

"Wait, let me guess!" Kyra interjected, turning to face Lacey. She held a hand up to her head. "Hmmm, let me see if I can guess your name in three tries. What do you think?"

"Yes! Guess! Guess!" Lacey cheered.

"Um, is your name Lily Lollipops?"

"No . . . !" Lacey giggled.

"Okay, let me try again . . ." Kyra tapped her temples with her fingers. "How about Pinky Puppydog?"

Lacey laughed even harder as she shook her head.

31

"Oh boy, this is my last guess!" Kyra said, pretending to look nervous. She crouched down so she was eye level with Lacey. "What if I guess wrong? What if —"

"I'm Lacey Chic!" Lacey cried, throwing her arms in the air.

JoJo, Goldie, and Kyra burst out laughing.

"It's very nice to meet you, Lacey Chic!" Kyra said as she stood back up. Lacey reached out and grabbed her hand. "You come see my room now," she cried as she tried to pull Kyra away.

"I think this playdate has officially begun!" Goldie exclaimed.

Two and a half hours later, JoJo was absolutely, positively exhausted.

"She has more energy than the Energizer Bunny," JoJo whispered to Kyra as she collapsed on a beanbag chair next to her. "And that's coming from someone whose nick-name is the Energizer Bunny!"

So far the girls had played Dress-up, Dinosaurs, Dance Party, and JoJo's absolute favorite . . . Dinosaur Dance Party. It had been Lacey's idea to combine the two. The rules were pretty simple—you had to pick your favorite dinosaur and then dance around the way that dinosaur would dance. After a few minutes of that, you'd collapse on the floor in giggles. The collapsing and giggling wasn't an official rule, but that was how the game had ended each of the three times the girls had played it.

In between all the playing, Lacey had insisted JoJo lip-synch along with some of her biggest hits while she danced around the room, trying to copy JoJo's moves.

"You sing 'Boom-rang' now!" Lacey cried, tugging on JoJo's arm.

"How about we do something quiet, like color?" Kyra replied, exchanging a wink with JoJo.

JoJo nodded gratefully. Usually she would never turn down an offer to perform, but she needed a break.

Lacey looked from JoJo to Kyra, and her face began to fall. Her lip began to tremble.

Uh-oh, this isn't good, JoJo thought.

"I have an idea!" she cried, jumping to her feet. "How about if YOU sing 'Boomerang' and dance for us? We can play Dance Competition, and Kyra and I will be judges!"

Lacey bit her lip, unsure of whether she wanted to do that. But then Kyra sprang into action, running over to the art table in the corner of the room. Grabbing a Magic Marker and a piece of construction paper, she quickly scrawled a "10" on the paper, surrounding it with hearts. She held the paper out for Lacey to see.

"Do you think you can get a perfect 10? I mean, it's really hard to do that, but I think you can do it . . ."

"I get 10!" Lacey cheered.

"And that, my friend, is how you do it." Kyra flicked her hair over her shoulder as JoJo walked over to where her phone was docked to turn the music back on.

"Okay, ready, Lacey? Here we go!"

JoJo pressed play, and Lacey began shimmying around the room. She didn't know all the words to JoJo's hit song "Boomerang," but she knew some. Watching her perform was one of the cutest things JoJo had ever seen. She loved that her music brought so much joy to others!

Midway through the song, Lacey pulled

JoJo and Kyra onto the makeshift dance floor with her.

JoJo and Kyra did their best to imitate her moves. They were all dancing around together when Goldie appeared at the door of the playroom, a huge smile on her face as she watched the performance.

When the song was finished, Goldie applauded. JoJo showed Lacey how to bow while Kyra ran over to grab the piece of paper with the 10 on it.

"The judges have decided that performance earned you a *perfect* 10!" Kyra cried, turning the sheet of paper over to show Lacey, who clapped in delight.

"I can see this has been the best playdate ever," Goldie said as Lacey ran over to her for a hug. "I can't thank you girls enough! I got so much work done these past few hours!"

"It was our pleasure!" JoJo replied.

"I hope she didn't wear you out so much that you won't do it again," Goldie replied as she ruffled Lacey's hair. "We'd *love* to do this again soon. Also, little miss has a birthday coming up, and I'm throwing a huge princess-themed party for her. I hope you can both make it!"

"I wouldn't miss it!" Kyra exclaimed.

"As long as I'm free that day, I'm in!" JoJo added.

"Great." Goldie nodded. "The party is next Sunday. I'm making her princess dress myself, of course. Actually, Kyra, I'd love to show you the design when I'm finished with it to see what you think! That would give us the chance to talk shop about designing, which I would also love to do!"

"That would be *fantastic!*" Kyra replied, her face lighting up. "How about tomorrow night?"

JoJo frowned. She knew Kyra was excited about the opportunity—it was *such* a great opportunity, after all—but she seemed to have forgotten about their sleepover with Grace and Miley. JoJo decided the right thing to do was to remind her. "Um, Kyra, tomorrow is our sleepover, remember?"

"How about Sunday, then?" Goldie replied smoothly. "I don't mean to rush you, but I'll need to start sewing early next week to have the dress done in time for the party . . ."

"Sunday works!" Kyra nodded eagerly.

"JoJo, can you join us?" Goldie asked. "I'm sure Lacey would love to see you again so soon! And I promise I won't let her tire you out quite so much next time!"

"I have to check my schedule when I get home," JoJo replied. "Don't get me wrong, I *love* hanging out with Lacey, but sometimes there are just not enough hours in the day to do all the stuff I want to do and sleep too . . ." JoJo sighed.

"I totally get it," Goldie said. "And same goes for you, Kyra. I know how busy you girls must be. If you can't come talk about the dress with me on Sunday, we'll just meet up another time to talk about your designs!"

"Sunday definitely works for me," Kyra replied confidently. "In fact, you've just given me an idea. I've always wanted to design a tiara, and now I have the perfect reason to do it!"

"Oh wow, did you hear that?" Goldie exclaimed, picking Lacey up and twirling her around. "Kyra's going to make you a special princess tiara for your birthday!"

CHAPTER 4

"**A**re we sure Kyra will be good with extra cheese, or should we wait for her to get here?" Miley asked.

It was Saturday night, and JoJo and Grace were at Miley's house. The girls were hanging out in Miley's room, watching TV, eating gummy bears, and picking out nail polish colors for the manicures they would give each other later.

Kyra had texted to say she was running a little late.

"I think extra cheese is a safe bet," Grace replied. "I know she can't wait to try this Maria's Pizza you've been raving about, so I don't think she'll be too picky about toppings. But I can text her to make sure."

"Unless we want to go with pineapple," JoJo said, gesturing to the TV.

"Pineapple?" Miley looked at JoJo like she had sprouted tentacles. "You know Kyra *hates* pineapple!"

JoJo burst out laughing. "I meant 'cause *SpongeBob* is on . . . you know, *who lives in a pineapple under the sea?*"

Miley and Grace dissolved into giggles. "You had me worried there for a moment," Miley teased.

"Hey, a lot of people swear by pineapple pizza," JoJo replied.

Just then the doorbell rang. BowBow sprang up from JoJo's lap and ran to the door.

"Such a good little watchdog," JoJo cooed.

Mr. McKenna's voice could be heard from downstairs welcoming Kyra, followed by a door slamming and Kyra's footsteps as she bounded up the stairs to Miley's room.

"Sorry I'm late!" Kyra exclaimed, tossing her cloud-printed overnight bag on Miley's bed. "I got into a groove working on tiara designs and lost track of time!"

"Tiara designs?" Grace raised her eyebrows. "I assumed you were working on your book report! But do tell!"

"Oh gosh, I have not even started on my book report yet!" Kyra replied as BowBow ran over to sniff her hands. JoJo wondered if

BowBow was smelling Kyra's pet miniature pig, Susie.

Kyra filled everyone in on her plan to make a special princess tiara for Lacey Chic for her princess-themed birthday party.

"But you haven't seen the dress design yet," JoJo said, patting the space next to her for BowBow to come lay down. "Can you design the tiara without seeing the dress first?"

"Sure." Kyra nodded. "Plus, I wanted to have some designs ready to show Goldie when I go over there tomorrow night to look at her dress design. Can you guys believe that Goldie asked me to consult on the design of Lacey's party dress? How amazing is that?"

"Extremely amazing," Miley replied as she pulled out her iPad and began scrolling through the menu for Maria's Pizza.

JoJo looked over at Grace and noticed she had her head down.

43

"What's wrong, Grace?" JoJo asked.

Grace looked up. "I just . . ." She cleared her throat and started again, her voice a little stronger this time. "Kyra, I thought we were going to work on our book reports together tomorrow night?"

Kyra's face fell as she realized she had upset her best friend. "Oh em gee, Grace, I am so sorry! I totally forgot we had plans!" She reached over and touched Grace's arm. "Seriously, I didn't mean to let you down! I can cancel on Goldie!"

JoJo watched the exchange between her two friends. She knew it used to be hard for Grace to speak up when something was bothering her, and she was glad that Grace was now comfortable doing so. It also made JoJo happy to see how supportive and thoughtful Kyra was being about Grace's feelings.

Grace shook her head firmly. "It's okay. This sounds like a great opportunity and you should do it. I'll just practice in front of the mirror like Miley suggested."

"Are you sure?" Kyra asked. "Because *nothing* comes before my friends! Not even fashion!"

JoJo smiled. She knew Kyra meant it.

"I'm sure," Grace replied, flashing her purple braces as she grinned. "But, as your friend, I will say that I'm a little worried because you have a *lot* to do. How are you going to design and make a tiara, collaborate with Goldie Chic on a princess dress, do your book report, and go to school and do all the other stuff you have to do, all at the same time?"

JoJo nodded. "She's right, Kyra. Maybe you are taking on too much with the tiara? I mean, what if Goldie asks us to babysit again? It sounds like she wants us to . . ."

Kyra looked a little uncertain for a moment, but then her face broke into a sunny smile. "Don't you guys worry about me! I'll make it work," she said confidently.

Later that night, after stuffing themselves on Maria's Pizza and giving each other manicures, JoJo and her friends were curled up on the floor of Miley's room, listening to music and waiting for their nails to dry.

"Do you think my nails are dry enough for gummy bears yet?" Grace asked, eyeing the half-empty bag on Miley's bed.

"I wouldn't risk it," JoJo advised. "Remember what happened that time with the cheesy puffs?"

"I don't think I'll ever forget." Grace grimaced as she remembered the time her purple ombré manicure ended up with bright orange cheese dust stuck to it. "Such a waste of a good mani!"

"But speaking of manicures, great job on mine, Miley," JoJo said, wiggling her rainbow-colored fingertips in front of her. BowBow raised her head and then sighed as if to say *Can't you pet me yet?*

"I love mine too," Miley replied. JoJo had painted Miley's nails pale pink and then had carefully drawn the letters M-I-L-E-Y in glitter, one on each finger of her left hand, to spell her name.

Just then, JoJo's phone pinged. She picked up her phone and carefully tapped the screen.

"It's Jacob," she said. "He wants to know if we can do a quick cupcake taste test tomorrow. He's still experimenting with raspberry flavors."

"I'm in, as long as it's quick, 'cause I have a ton of homework!" Miley said.

"Same." JoJo nodded. "My voice lessons are canceled next week because my coach had to go out of town, so I have some extra free time. Grace, how about you?"

"As much as I love Jacob's cupcakes, I really ought to focus on my book report," Grace replied after considering for a moment.

"I can't make it either." Kyra sighed. "Unless I can squeeze it in between going to Goldie's, designing the tiara, and working on my book report . . ."

"Kyra, it's okay to say no," JoJo said. "Jacob won't mind. I can just tell him you have a ton of stuff going on."

Kyra thought about it. "Okay, I guess I shouldn't. But please tell him I'm sorry!"

JoJo tapped out a quick reply to Jacob, and then a moment later turned her phone around so her friends could see the screen. Jacob had texted "K, cool!" followed by six cupcake emojis.

"See, he's fine with it," JoJo said.

"Plus, this means more cupcakes for JoJo and me!" Miley teased.

"Don't remind me!" Grace said, pretending to wipe a tear away. "I'd so much rather be eating cupcakes than working on my book report!"

"I think you made the right decision," JoJo told her. "And besides, you know we will save any leftovers for you!"

A few minutes later the girls decided their nails were finally dry enough for late-night snacks. Miley offered to make a kitchen run, and Grace said she'd go with her.

"In case you need help carrying our haul," Grace said with a laugh as she and Miley left the room.

"So . . . since you have some free time, does that mean you're going to come to Goldie's tomorrow?" Kyra asked JoJo.

"I'm going to pass," JoJo replied.

"Oh come on, JoJo!" Kyra said, giving JoJo her best puppy-dog eyes. "What if I get nervous? I'd feel much more confident if you were there with me!"

"I don't want to let you down, Kyra, but the idea of hanging with my family and catching up on homework and stuff like that tomorrow night sounds *really* good to me. I just want to lay low. Besides, you'll be fine on your own. Your confidence was totally on point when we babysat!"

"I guess that's true." Kyra sighed, and JoJo laughed.

Just then Kyra's phone dinged at the same time as JoJo's.

JoJo glanced at her screen first.

"It's Goldie," JoJo said a moment later. "She wants to know if we can come over Monday night to do something low-key like watch a movie with Lacey, because she has to have a business meeting at home."

"Ugh, I don't think I can do it!" Kyra cried, clearly frustrated. Then she bit her lip. JoJo could practically see the gears turning in her head. *"Or can I? Maybe I can get enough work done on my book report on Sunday night after I get back from Goldie's, and then I can stay up late finishing the tiara design . . ."*

"What's this?" Miley asked as she and Grace came back into the room, arms laden with chips, pretzels, and ice pops. JoJo filled them in on the text from Goldie.

"Grace, would you mind if I went to Goldie's again on Monday night, or should I save that night so we can work together on our reports?"

Grace tore open a bag of chips. "I wouldn't mind if you went to Goldie's," she said slowly. "You don't have to worry about me with the report—I'm really okay with working alone. But like I said before, what if you're taking on too much? *That's* what I am worried about."

"I agree," JoJo said, reaching for the bag of pretzels.

"I really don't want to let Goldie down." Kyra sighed. "Especially since she's going out of her way to include me in the dress design for Lacey."

"Well, I can probably go," JoJo replied, taking a bite of a pretzel. "I don't have a singing lesson on Monday night, so I don't have plans. If it would make you feel better, I'll go. Especially since I'm not going on Sunday."

"That would definitely make me feel better," Kyra replied gratefully. "But you have to promise to text me if the meeting is with another famous designer!"

"Deal," JoJo said. "Now someone hand me an ice pop before they melt!"

CHAPTER 5

Monday morning JoJo woke up feeling like a million bucks. She was glad she'd chosen to stay home the night before to have a "quiet" night with her family. They'd had a family game night, so it wasn't *quiet*, exactly— charades never were in the Siwa household— but it *was* a ton of fun.

After giving BowBow a good morning kiss on the head, JoJo headed downstairs to rustle up some breakfast. She had a busy day ahead of her! Schoolwork, a vlog recording, dance rehearsal, and then she'd end the day at Goldie's babysitting for Lacey.

I need some fuel, JoJo thought as she opened the fridge. She spotted the plate with the left-over cupcakes from Jacob's taste testing. *Must be a good friend and save for Grace and Kyra,* she reminded herself. It was hard to pass them up, though . . . Jacob had truly outdone him-self with this latest creation: raspberry swirl with a crumb topping.

JoJo pushed the cupcakes aside and pulled out ingredients for a healthy breakfast smoothie. She eyed the cupcakes one more time before closing the refrigerator door. She hoped Jacob would decide another round of taste testing was in order.

Before JoJo knew it, the day was over and she was walking up to Goldie Chic's house.

"JoJo, come in!" Goldie said as she opened the door and ushered her inside. She engulfed JoJo in a perfumed hug.

"Kyra and Lacey are already down in the playroom," Goldie said, expertly navigating the rugs in her high heels as she led JoJo through the hallway. "They loaded up on snacks, but let me know if you need anything!"

"Wait, did you say—"

"Oh, and so you're not confused when you get down there, my business partner Nathalia brought her two little ones over because her sitter canceled. But they play together really nicely with Lacey, so it should be all good!"

"Okay," JoJo said. She could tell Goldie was in a rush to get back to her meeting, so she didn't want to keep her. She'd just have to ask Kyra what she was doing here when she got downstairs.

But JoJo didn't have time to take her jacket off, let alone catch up with Kyra, when she got down to the playroom. The moment her foot hit the last step, Lacey spotted her and beelined over, hugging her so hard she almost knocked her down.

"Whoa!" JoJo cried, pretending to topple over. Lacey, of course, thought this was hilarious, as did the little girl who was standing next to her. Both girls jumped on top of JoJo.

"Help!" JoJo called. A moment later Kyra came to her rescue. JoJo quickly scrambled to her feet.

"JoJo, meet Mandy," Kyra said, pointing to a little girl with blond ringlets who looked to be about Lacey's age. "She's Lacey's buddy."

"Hi, Mandy." JoJo waved.

"And this is Jenna," Kyra said, pointing to a taller girl with the same curly blond hair as

Mandy but hers was in pigtails with matching bows.

"I'm five and a half," Jenna announced. "Mandy is only three and a half, so I'm the big sister, and I'm way more *mature*."

JoJo nodded and bit the inside of her cheek to keep from laughing. "It's nice to meet you! I'm JoJo. I love your bows!"

"Thanks, I like your bow too," Jenna said, gesturing to the rainbow-striped bow JoJo wore in her side pony.

"We are so happy you are here," Kyra said, pulling her into the room. Then she lowered her voice so only JoJo could hear. "Especially me—it's like a tornado *times three* down here!"

JoJo was just about to ask Kyra what she was doing there when Jenna grabbed her hand and pulled her to the center of the room.

"We were playing Dance Competition," Jenna explained. "But now it's our turn to be the judges and you have to dance!" She turned to Lacey and Mandy and pointed to some beanbag chairs against the wall. "Sit down and get ready to judge!"

JoJo couldn't believe how quickly they obeyed Jenna.

"The power of the big sister," she joked to Kyra.

Kyra laughed. "I've found it's best to do what Jenna says . . ."

"All right then," JoJo said, removing her jacket. "Let me just warm up . . ."

"No time for warming up!" Jenna replied. She walked over to the phone that was docked on the table and began to scroll. Moments later JoJo's hit song "Kid in a Candy Store" started playing *really* loud.

"Should we turn it down a bit since your moms are upstairs—" JoJo yelled, but Jenna cut her off.

"Dance!" Jenna ordered.

"Dance, dance!" Lacey and Mandy cheered.

Kyra shrugged.

So JoJo danced.

Eventually, after six songs, and mostly 10s but a few 8s (Jenna was a tough judge!), JoJo begged for a snack break.

"You're a really good dancer," Jenna said as she munched on carrots and hummus.

"Thanks!" JoJo smiled. "I love dancing! How about you?"

"I love cats," Jenna replied. "And I love being a big sister."

"Awwww!" JoJo and Kyra said in unison. Jenna was such a sweetheart.

"Jenna, could you help the little kids draw for a few minutes while I talk to Kyra?" JoJo asked after the snacks were finished. She knew that Lacey and Mandy needed to be kept occupied at all times, but she wanted to talk to Kyra.

Jenna tilted her head as she thought about it. "Okay," she said finally.

With that, Jenna marched over to Lacey and Mandy and told them it was time to draw. JoJo giggled as she watched Jenna escort them over to the drawing table and pull out construction paper and crayons from the nearby bins and point to the chairs she wanted them to sit in.

"She'd make a good babysitter," JoJo said as she and Kyra began cleaning up the plates from snack time.

"Or a drill sergeant," Kyra joked. "Totally kidding! I love how confident she is!"

"I agree," JoJo said. "She reminds me of a friend of mine . . ."

"Oh yeah?" Kyra asked. "Is this friend a super talented designer?"

"*Maybe,*" JoJo teased.

"Does she have purple streaks?" Kyra said, twirling one of her long, purple-streaked braids.

"*Maybe,*" JoJo said again. "Actually, yes, she does! And she also has me totally confused, because I thought I wasn't going to see her today since she was going to be working on her book report!" JoJo threw the last bits of garbage away and gestured to the beanbag chairs for Kyra to sit with her. "I'm thrilled to see you, but what's up? Did you pull an all-nighter and finish your book report last night?"

"Ugh, I wish," Kyra replied, plopping into a chair. "After I was here last night working on the dress design with Goldie—which was totally amazing, by the way—she invited me to stay for dinner, which turned into me staying to read Lacey a bedtime story. I was exhausted by the time I got home, but also super *energized* from Goldie's feedback on my tiara design, so I stayed up really late working on them and didn't do any work on my book report."

"Them? As in more than one?" JoJo asked. She looked over at the art table. The girls were calmly drawing, and Jenna seemed to have a handle on everything.

"I'll get to that in a second," Kyra said. "So anyway, today I dropped by after school to show Goldie the changes I made last night. I *was* going to tell her I couldn't sit tonight, but then her partner called and asked about bringing her kids to the meeting. I heard Goldie tell her she'd have two helpers here—me and you—so I *couldn't* cancel."

"I appreciate you being here . . . ," JoJo said

slowly. "But you didn't have to stay. If three kids were too much for me, I would have spoken up!"

"That's the thing." Kyra sighed. "I *want* to be here. I love babysitting, and it's even more fun with you! And besides . . . what if Goldie wants to talk about design stuff with me again?"

"I know it's hard to choose not-so-fun stuff over the fun stuff," JoJo said sympathetically. "*Believe me*, I understand. I miss out on going to school with you, Miley, Grace, and Jacob, but being homeschooled allows me to do all the other things that are really important to me. It all balances out. But you have to work to find that balance, and sometimes that means saying no to some of the fun stuff so you can do the *important* stuff."

"I know, you're right," Kyra said. "You're a wise one, JoJo Siwa!"

"I know," JoJo replied, pretending to bow. "But now what's the deal with the tiaras? As in *more than one?*"

"Well . . ." Kyra sank deeper into her bean-bag chair. "Goldie told her partner about the one I'm making for Lacey, and Nathalia offered to pay me to make tiaras for Mandy and Jenna to wear to the party. How could I say no to that?"

JoJo groaned. "That's wonderful—it truly is—but now you have to make *three* tiaras, finish a book report, rehearse presenting the report, and do all your other homework all at the same time?"

Kyra nodded.

"When is the book report due?" JoJo asked.

"A week from today."

"And the party is Sunday, right?" JoJo replied.

Kyra nodded again.

"Sounds like you're going to need to make a schedule and stick to it," JoJo said. "And let me know if I can help. I'm here for you, you know!"

"I know you are." Kyra smiled appreciatively. "But I'll be fine—I'll figure it out!"

Just then, there was a commotion at the arts table.

JoJo and Kyra ran over to see what was happening. Lacey had accidentally broken Mandy's purple crayon.

"I think drawing time is over," JoJo said. "What's next?"

"How about a dance party?" Jenna asked.

"Dance! Dance!" Lacey and Mandy cheered, the purple crayon forgotten.

"Okay, okay!" JoJo laughed. Then she had an idea. "Maybe Kyra can work on her homework while we dance? Would that be okay?"

"Sure," Jenna replied as she turned the music on really, really loud once again.

"Can we turn it down a bit so Kyra can work?" JoJo had to shout to be heard.

"You can't have quiet music at a dance party," Jenna replied.

Kyra giggled and joined JoJo in the middle of the floor. "I can't argue with that," she agreed. "And besides"—she cupped a hand over her mouth so just JoJo could hear her—"like I said before, it's best to listen to Jenna!"

CHAPTER 6

It was Tuesday afternoon, and JoJo was taking a much needed study break when she heard her phone ping. And then it pinged two more times. She glanced at the clock and realized it was after 3 P.M., which meant her friends were done with school for the day. It was a pretty safe bet that someone had started a group chat!

Sure enough, Jacob had texted JoJo, Miley, Grace, and Kyra to see if anyone was free for one last cupcake taste test. JoJo grabbed her phone and began to catch up on the group text.

JACOB: *Who's in for cupcake tasting Part 3?*

MILEY: *YES PLZ!*

GRACE: *Me! I need a break! My place in an hour?*

JoJo grinned as typed her response.

JOJO: *I'm in! Tho I can't imagine how you're gonna top those crumb cupcakes cuz those were delish!*

JoJo realized that Kyra hadn't yet responded, but that was probably because she was hard at work on her book report. Maybe she had even turned her phone off to avoid distractions. *Good for you, Kyra,* JoJo thought.

An hour later, JoJo and BowBow arrived at Grace's house at the same time as Jacob, who was carrying a big, round container that JoJo recognized as his cupcake carrier.

"Need me to take those off your hands?" JoJo joked.

"Ha ha." Jacob grinned as he rang the doorbell. "I can't wait for you to try this new flavor!"

A moment later Mrs. Taylor opened the door and welcomed JoJo, BowBow, and Jacob inside. "Miley and Grace are out back," she said, pointing to the sliding glass door off the kitchen. "Do you want BowBow to go with you or stay in here with us?"

"I think BowBow will want to be wherever Georgie is, isn't that right?" JoJo asked BowBow, who wagged her tail so hard at the sound of Georgie's name that it looked like she was dancing.

"Out back it is, then!" Mrs. Taylor laughed.

BowBow got so excited when she saw Georgie that she almost slipped out of her collar. "Hang on, BowBow!" JoJo cried, bending down to unclip the leash from BowBow's collar so she could run off to greet her puppy pal.

JoJo walked over to the table and said hello to Miley and Grace as Jacob began to transfer delicious-looking cupcakes from the container to a large plate.

"How's the book report coming?" JoJo asked Grace as she sank into a chair.

"I was just telling Miley it's all done, and I've been practicing a lot in the mirror!" Grace replied. "I took your tip, JoJo, and recorded myself and that helped a lot too. I never realized how much I say *ummm*!"

"I never noticed that about you," JoJo said reassuringly.

"Thanks." Grace smiled. "Which brings me to . . . I think I'm almost ready for an audience. Any chance I can practice in front of you guys on Saturday night?"

"Sure!" JoJo said after doing a quick run-through of her schedule in her head. "I'm free! Want to do it at my house?"

"That would be great," Grace replied gratefully.

"I'm in too!" Miley said.

"Me three," Jacob added. "I'll be done baking by then since the shower is on Saturday, so count me in!"

"Thanks so much, you guys," Grace said with a smile as she leaned back in her chair. "Kyra has been checking in with me nonstop. I know she feels really badly about not being available to work on our reports together, so I don't want to add anything to her plate by making her feel like she has to rehearse with me. Not when I have you guys to fill in!"

"That's what we're here for." JoJo smiled. "And speaking of Kyra, has anyone heard from her?"

"Actually, no," Grace said as Miley and Jacob shook their heads. "But I was thinking maybe she shut her phone off so she could work."

"I was thinking the same thing," JoJo said. "Well, good for her! I know she was pretty stressed yesterday about all the stuff she has to get done this week. We'll just have to make sure to save a cupcake for her—"

"Actually, there's no need to, I'm here!"

JoJo, Miley, Grace, and Jacob all looked up to see Kyra walking toward them.

"I can explain!" Kyra laughed as she plopped into a chair. "I figured out a way to do the tiaras that will be less time consuming, and last night I made some pretty good progress on my book report. So I decided I deserved a cupcake break! Plus, Jacob, this will be quick, right?"

"Quick and delicious!" Jacob replied.

"That's great news about your report," Grace said. "What's the new plan for the tiaras? I know you were saying how it can take hours to make just one. What changed?"

"Well, I found this special glue online that will give me a lot more flexibility when I'm placing the crystals on the tiaras, which is one of the most time-consuming parts because it can be hard to get them to lay just right when they are all lined up. This glue dries more slowly, so I can really take my time and fix little mistakes as I go. Not that I'm planning to make a bunch of mistakes," she added with a grin.

"Using new supplies always makes me nervous," Grace said. "I remember one time I had to use waterproof paint and it ended up being really gloppy. I was able to thin it out with paint thinner, but it was a pain."

"I didn't even think about that," Kyra admitted.

"I'm sure it will be fine," Grace said reassuringly. "You know me, I *always* think about stuff like that!"

"And I am the queen of not thinking about that stuff!" Kyra laughed. "I still need to figure out the final shape for each tiara so I can construct them from wire. Goldie gave me awesome advice when she looked at my sketches. I have Lacey's all figured out, but I still need to draw up a final design for the other two. That's the part I am the most worried about, but you can't rush genius."

"It sounds like you still have a lot to do, even with this new glue helping to save some time," JoJo commented.

"I do, but I'll get it all done." Kyra smiled confidently.

"You'll 'make it happen'?" JoJo teased, quoting Goldie Chic.

"Exactly," Kyra replied.

"On that note, can we get down to cupcake business?" Jacob said, placing the plate of cupcakes at the center of the table. "My latest and greatest new creation is . . . raspberry hazelnut! I need to decide today what flavor I am making once and for all, so I can shop for all the ingredients tomorrow after school and start baking."

The girls all helped themselves to a cupcake.

JoJo carefully peeled back the paper and looked closely at the cupcake before taking her first bite. "It looks really pretty," she commented. "I love the swirly design on the icing." JoJo knew Jacob was capable of doing some pretty intricate patterns and designs with frosting, but she liked how elegant and simple this icing was. It seemed perfect for a bridal shower!

JoJo closed her eyes and took a bite, careful to get frosting *and* cake so she could taste everything together. She loved the crunch of the hazelnuts and the tang of the raspberry jelly in the center. The cupcake was, in short, absolutely scrumptious.

"So good," she sighed a moment later.

"Better than the crumb ones?" Jacob asked.

"Um . . ." JoJo couldn't decide. "Help me out, guys!" she cried.

"I think I'd vote for the crumb," Miley said. "I mean . . . I think? Maybe? Actually, I'm not sure!"

"No, you said crumb, so that counts as a vote for crumb!" Jacob said, wagging a finger at Miley. "No take-backs!"

The girls all laughed.

"I still really love the peanut butter swirl flavor the best," Grace said. "Sorry, Jacob!"

"I think this is my favorite," Kyra said. She took another bite and concentrated as she chewed. "Yep, this is the winner for me."

"So we have one vote for the hazelnut, one vote for the peanut butter swirl, and one vote for the crumb-topped. JoJo, it's up to you to cast the deciding vote!"

"Pressure's on!" Miley teased.

"I'll do what I did last time," Jacob said, leaning forward in his chair. "I'll ask you, and you tell me the first one that pops into your head. Ready? *Which flavor is best?*"

"I like them all!" JoJo blurted out.

Everyone burst out laughing, except for Jacob, who groaned.

"I'm so sorry, Jacob," JoJo said. "It's a tie for

me between those three. They are all so good but so different! I can't choose!"

"It's too bad you can't make all three," Grace mused.

"Wait a second . . . ," Jacob replied, tapping his fingers on the table. "I can, though! The base batter is the same for all three. I could actually make all three variations using the same vanilla batter. I'd just add the peanut butter swirl to one batch, the crumb topping to a second batch, and the hazelnut crunch to a third batch!"

"It sounds to me like you have a winner then!" JoJo cheered. "Or make that three winners!"

As everyone helped themselves to lemonade to wash down the cupcakes, Kyra suddenly snapped her fingers. "I just had the best idea, inspired by Jacob's cupcakes!" she cried. "I'll use the same basic tiara design for all three tiaras—the one I already drew up for Lacey—and just vary the placement and pattern of the crystals so they are each unique!"

"That's brilliant!" JoJo cheered.

"I knew I made the right choice coming today!" Kyra laughed. JoJo noticed she suddenly looked much more relaxed. .

"So what you're really saying . . . ," Jacob said, "is that my cupcakes saved the day. Am I right?"

"I'd like to propose a toast," JoJo said, raising her glass of lemonade. "To baked goods saving the day!"

CHAPTER 7

The rest of the week flew by for JoJo. Her favorite part of the week, aside from seeing her friends, was making a new video to post on YouTube starring BowBow.

Now it was Friday night, and Goldie had invited JoJo and Kyra out for manicures as a special thank-you for babysitting.

As Goldie walked up to the nail salon, pushing Lacey's stroller, JoJo heard Kyra gasp excitedly.

"JoJo, don't look now, but Goldie is wearing the same exact sneakers as me!" Kyra whispered.

JoJo looked and, sure enough, Goldie Chic was wearing the same teal low-top sneakers with butterflies stitched on the sides that Kyra had on.

"Why are you whispering?" JoJo giggled.

"Well, I don't want to *announce* it! If she happens to notice, great, but I'm not going to point it out . . ."

But the moment Goldie joined the girls, showing off her new sneakers was the second thing she did. The first thing she did was give both girls a hello hug.

"Do you like my new kicks?" she asked, extending one foot and wiggling it to show off her shoe. "I took some fashion inspiration from one of my favorite up-and-coming designers," she added, winking at Kyra.

"Wow, you knew I have those?" Kyra squealed.

Goldie laughed. "Of course! I noticed you wearing them, and I thought they were super cute. I found them online. I hope you don't mind if we're twinning . . ."

"MIND?" Kyra exclaimed. "I'm incredibly flattered!"

Just then, JoJo heard a whimpering sound coming from the stroller. In all their excitement over Goldie's sneakers, they had forgotten to say hello to Lacey, and she looked ready to dissolve into tears. Luckily JoJo knew just what to do.

"Where's Lacey?" she asked, pretending to look around.

"What? She's—" Kyra started to respond, but then she caught on. "Hmm, I don't see her. Goldie, did you forget someone very important?"

JoJo heard Lacey giggle.

"As excited as I am to get a mani, the *real* reason I'm here is to see Lacey!" JoJo said. "I'm going home if she's not here . . ."

"Me too!" Kyra added. "Where, oh where, can she be?"

"I RIGHT HERE!" Lacey yelled, erupting into giggles.

"How did we not see you?" JoJo cried. "Did you turn invisible?"

Lacey continued to giggle, and once she started clapping too, JoJo knew they were in the clear.

"I don't know what I would do without you guys," Goldie said. "You are so good with her!"

Inside the nail salon, Goldie, Lacey, JoJo, and Kyra checked out the huge selection of nail polish colors.

"I've never seen so much nail polish in my life," JoJo commented.

"It's like your bow collection," Kyra said with a laugh.

It was true; JoJo had a huge collection of bows at home. She had a bow for every outfit and every occasion. As did BowBow!

"Hey, you can never have too many bows," JoJo said.

"Especially not when they are your signature accessory," Goldie agreed. "It's like me with scarves. And hats. And chunky bracelets. And let's face it . . . basically every accessory!"

"Same!" Kyra said while reaching for a bottle of polish to take a closer look.

"Okay, accessory masters, what do you think of this shade of pink, maybe with a coat of silver glitter on top?" JoJo held the two bottles of nail polish next to each other.

"Hold the pink one against the top of your hand so we can see if it works with your skin tone," Goldie advised.

JoJo followed Goldie's advice, and wrinkled her nose. She didn't love it.

"Try this one," Goldie suggested, pointing to a bottle of pink polish that was very similar to the one JoJo had chosen, but a little less peachy.

"Much better," JoJo said as she held that shade up to her hand.

"Let me see!" Lacey cried from her stroller. JoJo showed the two bottles to Lacey, who grinned her approval.

"What do you think of this color?" Kyra asked. She held out a shimmering, opalescent shade of blue.

"It reminds me of a mermaid," JoJo said. "And that's a good thing!"

"I agree! Excellent choice," Goldie said. "You've got great taste, girl."

JoJo and Kyra helped Lacey select her color . . . which was actually ten colors, because she wanted to paint each nail a different rainbow color. She picked the ten brightest colors in the polish collection, including a few neon shades.

"Are you sure you don't want to go with a pastel color to match your princess dress for your party?" Goldie asked her.

"Rainbow!" Lacey insisted, shaking her head.

"Rainbow it is then!" Goldie shrugged.

JoJo smiled. She loved that, as young as she was, Lacey had opinions and that Goldie had no problem letting her sport nails that might not match perfectly with her princess dress. As far as JoJo was concerned, everyone should wear whatever made them feel good! She was happy to see that Goldie seemed to think so too.

JoJo and Kyra settled into their chairs across from their manicurists. The manicurist who would be doing Goldie's and Lacey's nails was running a little late.

"How about if Lacey and I dash over there and get us some frozen deliciousness to enjoy while we're getting pampered?" Goldie suggested, gesturing to the coffee shop next door.

"I'm not going to say no to that!" JoJo replied.

"Same," Kyra agreed.

Goldie took their drink orders. "JoJo, that's extra whip and caramel sauce? Are you sure that's enough sugar?" she teased.

"There's no such thing as enough sugar!" JoJo joked.

"Tell me about it," Kyra sighed as Goldie left with Lacey to go next door. "I barely slept last night, and I'm so tired today. And I have another late night ahead of me tonight."

"Working on the book report?" JoJo asked.

"Not even," Kyra replied. "I haven't worked on it since Sunday night, and now I'm way behind schedule. But the good news is, the tiaras are pretty much done. I finished setting all of the stones last night." She turned to face JoJo. "That new glue didn't save as much time as I thought. I still had to draw out detailed plans for each design, and that took *forever*."

"Please stop moving," the manicurist said.

"Sorry," Kyra said, turning away from JoJo. "My plan is to put the finishing touches on the tiaras tonight after I get home, then finish reading my book before bed, and then spend all day tomorrow working on the report. I guess I'll rehearse my presentation on Sunday night after Lacey's party."

"That's cutting it pretty close," JoJo remarked. The manicurist finished filing the nails on JoJo's right hand and gently placed it in a bowl of warm soapy water.

"Can't you just be done with the tiaras, even if they're not absolutely perfect, so you can focus on your reading tonight? To give yourself a little wiggle room, just in case?" JoJo asked.

Kyra looked at her like she had just suggested she ride her bike to the moon.

"Hear me out," JoJo said, laughing at the expression on Kyra's face. "You said the tiaras are pretty much done, right? Maybe it's time to focus on your book report. I'm sure the tiaras look wonderful!"

"No way." Kyra shook her head, much to the annoyance of her manicurist. "Sorry! I'll stop moving now! But anyway, they have to be *perfect!*"

"But what about your report?" JoJo pressed. "Don't you want it to be perfect—or as close to perfect as possible—too?"

"It will be," Kyra said firmly. But then she yawned.

JoJo admired Kyra's determination, but she could see that her friend was being spread too thin. She also knew that when Kyra made up her mind about something, there was no changing it. All she could do was remind her that she was there to help if she needed anything.

"So Miley and Jacob are coming over tomorrow night to help Grace rehearse," JoJo reminded Kyra. "But please text us if you need anything . . ."

"I'll be fine—" Kyra began.

"I mean it," JoJo said, gently cutting her off. "You have a crazy schedule over the next two days, and if anything goes wrong, you're going to need help. Promise me you'll ask for help if you need it."

"I promise," Kyra said. From the expression on her face, JoJo could tell that Kyra had no intention of asking for help. But she could also tell how much Kyra appreciated the offer.

The door to the nail salon opened, and JoJo saw Goldie sweep back in, clutching a cardboard box filled with tall, icy drinks. Lacey—happily in tow—held onto her mother's free hand.

"Let's talk about something else," Kyra whispered to JoJo. "I don't want Goldie to know I'm such a mess with everything!"

"You are *not* a mess!" JoJo protested. Then she lowered her voice. "Goldie might be the perfect person to talk about this with. I mean, she's juggling a million things at once too. I'm sure she knows what it's like to be overwhelmed."

"I doubt that," Kyra sighed. "She's got it all figured out. She's a famous designer about to launch her new spring line, and she still manages to plan a huge party, design a party dress, and mentor me on designs. She's not simply my fashion idol . . . I want to be just like her when I grow up."

JoJo agreed that Goldie was incredible, but she also knew that she probably had days when she wasn't on top of everything. No one could be perfect all the time. Not to mention that Goldie seemed to be pretty good at asking for help when she needed it. That was one important lesson JoJo hoped Kyra could learn from her idol.

CHAPTER 8

JoJo spent Saturday morning and afternoon practicing new dance routines. Having her voice lessons canceled for the past week had opened up a lot of time in her schedule—time that she knew she wouldn't have open again next week. It had been a nice change of pace, having extra time to see her friends and to babysit Lacey, but she was excited to get back to her vocal lessons next week. Next to dancing, singing was her true passion, and JoJo didn't mind putting in all the hard work that was necessary to pursue her dreams. She actually thrived on it.

Now it was early on Saturday evening, and JoJo, Miley, Grace, and Jacob were settling into the rec room in JoJo's basement. JoJo had cleared a spot at the front of the room for Grace to present her report, and she had set out bowls of popcorn and bottles of flavored sparkling water on the coffee table.

"There are plenty more snacks upstairs," JoJo said. "My mom did a grocery store run, so we're stocked up on candy, chips, and pretzels."

"Popcorn is perfect," Miley said, grabbing a handful. "It's like being at the movies!"

"Oh great, my book report has to live up to a movie?" Grace groaned.

"Just get up there and do your best," JoJo said, laughing.

"That's right," Jacob cheered. "Think of us as movie critics instead of an audience . . . wait, that didn't help, did it?"

"Definitely not helping!" JoJo teased, throwing a pillow at Jacob.

"Any last-minute tips before I begin?" Grace asked.

JoJo could tell Grace was nervous from the way she was clutching her report and pacing back and forth. She knew they needed to help Grace relax.

"I think the best advice I've gotten about performing is to remember to smile," JoJo said. "If you look like you're having a good time, everyone else will too."

"And I think you're supposed to make eye contact with members of the audience while you're speaking," Miley added.

"Ugh, I don't know if I can do that," Grace fretted. "Do I have to? Won't I look weird doing that?" To prove her point, Grace stared intently at each of her friends, not blinking, until everyone dissolved into laughter.

"Okay, not like that," JoJo said. "More like this . . ."

JoJo sprang from the couch, stood at the front of the room, and pretended to give a speech, right off the top of her head.

"Hi! I'm JoJo Siwa, and I'm here to tell you all about my dog, BowBow, who is the best dog in the world!" JoJo paused to glance at Grace and smile.

"Not only is BowBow adorable, she's got incredible fashion sense—just look at the pink rhinestone bow she's sporting tonight!"

JoJo gestured to BowBow, who had lifted her head up from her spot on the couch, as if on cue. She seemed to be listening to JoJo's speech. "She likes long walks on her leash and playing with other pups, especially Georgie the corgi!"

JoJo made eye contact with Jacob for a moment and smiled. "Her favorite snack is potato chips, but she's also a huge fan of vanilla ice cream, and she probably wouldn't turn down some popcorn if anyone wants to give her some . . ."

JoJo looked at Miley and grinned. She'd made the rounds and looked at everyone in her audience. "Thank you for taking the time today to listen to me talk about BowBow!" JoJo finished speaking and bowed dramatically while her friends applauded.

"You make that look way too easy," Grace said. But she was smiling, and she looked less nervous. *Mission accomplished*, JoJo thought.

"I think you're ready," JoJo said encouragingly as she settled back on the couch next to BowBow. "Just go for it, and if you make a mistake, keep going!"

"Okay, here goes nothing," Grace said, walking to the front of the room clutching her report.

JoJo listened carefully while Grace read her book report. The report was really interesting—it made JoJo want to read the book Grace was talking about. Grace made sure not to give the ending away, which JoJo appreciated. She spoke about the characters she liked the most and why. She stumbled a few times while she was speaking, but after JoJo, Miley, and Jacob smiled and nodded, she found her place and kept going.

When she was finished, JoJo, Miley, and Jacob broke into applause.

"You guys, it wasn't *that* good!" Grace protested, but she was grinning shyly.

"It was actually really good, especially for your first time," JoJo assured her. "Now go again!"

Grace nodded, cleared her throat, and began again.

For the next half hour or so, Grace practiced reading her report aloud. After each performance, JoJo, Miley, and Jacob would give her feedback. JoJo could see Grace growing more and more confident. By the fifth or sixth time she read the report, her smile came naturally and she had no problem looking up from the page and making eye contact with the "audience."

"Grace, you're practically a professional public speaker at this point," Miley said. Grace had just finished a flawless reading of the report, and they were all taking a break.

"I think I'm definitely comfortable giving the report in front of you guys," Grace said. "I'm not sure what will happen when I'm standing up in front of my class, but this helped a lot!"

"You're going to do great," JoJo assured her. But her brain was going a hundred miles an hour as she thought about what Grace had said. Presenting the report in front of her whole class was different than presenting it in front of her best friends. JoJo wished she could gather a group of people Grace didn't know who she could practice in front of.

Just then, JoJo's phone rang. Her phone rarely rang—everyone usually texted her. She pulled out her phone and saw that it was Kyra calling.

"It's Kyra," she announced.

"Maybe she's going to come over?" Jacob suggested.

"She'd just text that," Miley said.

JoJo answered the phone and sank into the couch, her friends gathered around, trying to figure out what was going on.

It was a quick conversation, but everyone could tell from the frown on JoJo's face that something was wrong.

"Kyra, I'm glad you called. Let me talk to everyone here and we'll get right back to you. Don't worry—it's going to be okay!" JoJo ended the call and explained to her friends what was happening.

"So Kyra went to Goldie's tonight to drop off the tiaras. She'd packaged them carefully in tissue paper, but when she got there, the stones had all popped off . . ."

"That new glue she used!" Grace groaned.

JoJo nodded. "Exactly. But it gets worse. Goldie accidentally took the wrong measurements for Lacey's dress, and she realized tonight it doesn't fit her at all. She has to redo almost the whole dress, and Kyra wants to help her, but . . ."

"But her tiaras need to be fixed," Miley finished.

JoJo nodded again. "And, to make matters even more complicated, Goldie's business partner, Nathalia, has her girls sleeping over at Goldie's tonight, so Goldie and Kyra have their hands full with three little girls who are too excited about tomorrow's princess party to let them get anything done."

"So basically, Kyra needs our help," Jacob said.

"Exactly," JoJo replied. "And she actually asked for it, which is kind of huge for her. What do you guys say?"

"I say we head over there right now," Grace said, jumping to her feet.

"I'll grab the snacks," Jacob said. "And, JoJo, I'll go let your mom know we need a ride over to Goldie's . . ."

"Thanks, Jacob," JoJo responded with a nod.

"Grace, are you sure you've practiced enough?" Miley asked.

"Definitely," Grace replied as she carefully placed her report in her backpack and zipped it closed. "What I probably need to do at this point is practice in front of an audience of people who aren't my best friends . . . but that's not going to happen! So let's go help our other best friend out of the jam she's in!"

As everyone raced around gathering up their stuff, an idea popped into JoJo's head.

"Grace, I think I know of a way you can practice in front of a new audience. How do you feel about rehearsing in front of three miniature judges . . . ?"

CHAPTER 9

On the way over to Goldie's house, JoJo explained her plan.

"Jacob, since you're the cake decorating master, you can take the lead on redoing the tiaras," JoJo began. "The stones need to be reglued onto the tiaras in the same pattern as before, but with better glue."

"I'll do whatever I can to help, but glue and crystals aren't exactly the same thing as icing and sprinkles," Jacob replied nervously.

"True, but I have faith in you!" JoJo said.

"And I can help," Grace volunteered. Grace was a fantastic artist and an obvious choice to help with the tiaras, but JoJo had something else in mind for her.

"Actually, you'll be helping to babysit *while* rehearsing your book report," JoJo said.

"Wait, what?" Grace asked. "Aren't these *little* kids we're babysitting for?"

"They may be little, but they have strong opinions," JoJo replied. "They loved being judges when we played Dance Competition, and trust me when I tell you, they will give you honest feedback on your report!"

"Um, watching you dance is way more entertaining than listening to my book report," Grace protested. "How are three little kids going to sit through that?"

JoJo grinned. "You'll understand when you meet Jenna!"

"Okay, so that leaves me," Miley said. "Should I work with Jacob on the tiaras?"

"That's what I was going to suggest," JoJo replied as her mom's car pulled into Goldie's driveway. "Sound good?"

"Sure!" Miley nodded as they scrambled out of the car. "Hopefully I'll discover some hidden tiara-making skills I never knew I had!"

"Oh, thank goodness you're here!" Goldie exclaimed a moment later as she opened the door to welcome JoJo and the others inside. "Welcome to Disaster Central . . . anything that can go wrong *has* gone wrong!"

"Reinforcements are here!" JoJo cried. She quickly introduced Goldie to Jacob and Grace.

JoJo had never seen Goldie look so frazzled. She'd actually never seen Goldie look anything other than flawlessly put together, but tonight was different. Her usually perfectly styled hair was in a messy ponytail, and she was dressed in plain sweats. But she was still smiling.

Goldie explained that Kyra was down in the playroom watching the girls. "She's got her hands full, but I've been scrambling to redo the dress," Goldie sighed. "You'd think that after doing this professionally for so long, I'd be able to make a dress without messing up the measurements, but that's *exactly* what I did!"

"Mistakes happen," JoJo said.

"Absolutely they do!" Goldie agreed as she led JoJo, Grace, Jacob, and Miley toward the door to the playroom. "I was just talking about that with Kyra. The poor girl is so upset about the tiaras, and I was telling her, *stuff happens.* You have to just roll with it!"

JoJo and the others made their way downstairs. It was suspiciously quiet and dark when they reached the playroom.

"Um, Kyra, everything okay down here?" JoJo asked, fumbling for the light switch.

"THANK GOODNESS you guys are here!" Kyra exclaimed, echoing what Goldie had said a few minutes earlier.

JoJo turned the lights on and looked around. Mandy, Lacey, and Jenna were curled up on the floor, pretending to be asleep. Lacey opened one eye, spotted JoJo, and began to wiggle with excitement.

"No moving!" Jenna warned.

"What's going on?" JoJo asked.

"Okay, wake up," Kyra said wearily. Jenna, Mandy, and Lacey sprang up from the floor and ran over to JoJo.

"We were playing Freeze Sleep," Kyra explained. "It's like Freeze Tag, but quieter . . . and calmer. Don't judge me," she said, holding up a hand as Jacob started to comment. "I was desperate. And I was hoping it would make them actually fall asleep, but as you can see"—she pointed to the three girls who were climbing all over JoJo—"they are not tired."

"Well, we got here just in time then," JoJo said. She pulled herself away from the giggling girls. "And we have a plan!"

"So do I," Kyra replied. She began pacing around the room. "I finished my book report yesterday, thank goodness, so at least that's done. Now that you're here, I'll help Goldie with the dress, and then tonight I'll stay up fixing the tiaras, and then—"

JoJo, Miley, Grace, and Jacob exchanged a look.

"Did you hear what I said?" JoJo said, putting a hand on Kyra's shoulder. "We have a plan! And you are going to let us help!"

It wasn't easy to convince Kyra that she didn't have to do everything by herself, but eventually JoJo, Grace, Miley, and Jacob managed to do just that.

Jacob and Miley set up shop at the arts and crafts table with all of Kyra's tiara-making supplies. Kyra showed them her designs and demonstrated how to glue on the stones. They got the hang of it quickly, especially Jacob, who said it was actually pretty similar to working with frosting.

Meanwhile, JoJo explained to Jenna that she needed her, Mandy, and Lacey to listen to Grace's book report and provide feedback. "Sort of like being a Dance Competition judge, but instead you're judging a book report," JoJo told her.

Jenna nodded and got to work, pulling the beanbag chairs to the front of the room where Grace was. She instructed Lacey and Mandy to sit down, and they did.

"This girl has to give a report in front of

her whole class on Monday, and we have to make sure she does a good job!" Jenna announced.

Mandy and Lacey nodded obediently.

"Okay, you can start now," Jenna said as she pointed to Grace.

"I'm a little scared of her," Grace whispered to JoJo.

"I promise, you're in good hands." JoJo laughed. She walked over to Kyra.

"I'm going to stay down here to help whoever needs me. But before you go upstairs, I wanted to see how you're doing. You okay?"

"I am." Kyra nodded. "I just can't *believe* I messed up the tiaras!"

"You didn't mess up!" JoJo exclaimed. "Like Goldie said, *stuff happens,* and you just have to roll with it!"

"I know, you're right." Kyra nodded again. "Thank you."

"Everyone has been asking me if she's here to perform, but she's here as a guest . . ."

The crowd rumbled. Some of the kids started chanting, "JoJo! JoJo!"

"This was totally unplanned." Goldie laughed nervously and looked over at JoJo. "But maybe we can convince her to sing one song for us later?"

"Sure, why not!" JoJo agreed, loud enough so everyone could hear.

"Yes!" Goldie cheered as the crowd erupted. "And this is my girl, Kyra," she continued. "Kyra helped create the dress Lacey is wearing, and she also designed the tiaras that Lacey, Mandy, and Jenna are wearing . . ." Goldie paused while everyone applauded.

"And last but not least, we have Grace, Jacob, and Miley. Last night they came over to help me out when I was in over my head with pre-party drama. This is one special

"Don't mention it! Now you get up there and show your idol your incredible sewing skills," JoJo said, giving Kyra a playful shove. "We've got everything under control down here."

"Do you, though?" Kyra asked. She pointed across the room to where Grace had just finished reading her book report. "I think Judge Jenna just gave Grace a 4 . . ."

"Oh no!" JoJo cried. "Jenna, let's talk about how you can help Grace with *constructive* feedback . . ."

It was Sunday afternoon, and Lacey's princess party was underway. Kyra was practically bursting with excitement because the guest list was a who's who of famous designers and fashion insiders.

Lacey looked adorable in her princess dress, which fit just right and featured the stitching work of the one and only Kyra Gregory. Her princess tiara had also turned out perfectly, as had Mandy's and Jenna's. And after they'd finished sewing the dress the night before, Goldie had spent the rest of the evening looking at Kyra's design portfolio and giving her feedback. She'd also promised Kyra she was available to her any time she wanted to get together and talk about her designs and career aspirations. Goldie was turning out to be a true mentor for Kyra.

Jacob ended up being so good at tiara making that he'd announced he was going to make a tiara-shaped cake as his next cake design challenge.

Grace, who had received super helpful feedback from her miniature judges, was feeling so confident about delivering her book report the next day that she'd taken the afternoon off to come to the party. All of JoJo's friends had come, as Goldie had practically insisted that they attend after helping out so much the night before.

Just then, Goldie clapped her hands and invited everyone into the backyard, where a stage had been set up for the entertainment that was happening later. There was also a sparkling juice fountain, a wishing well, and the largest castle-shaped bouncy house JoJo had ever seen.

Goldie walked onto the stage and smiled at the crowd gathered around her.

"Before we get to games and all that good stuff, I wanted to introduce some special friends," Goldie began. "JoJo, Kyra, Miley, Grace, and Jacob, can you guys come here?"

JoJo and her friends made their way up t the stage.

"I'm sure most of you know who JoJo Si is . . ." Goldie paused as the crowd cheer group of kids, and Lacey and I just love them to pieces!"

The crowd cheered. Goldie smiled as she waited for them to quiet down.

"So, to say thank you, I want to give them something from my new collection—these scarves are not even in stores until next year!" Goldie turned to face JoJo and her friends as Nathalia walked onstage and handed her a box filled with fancy gift bags. "You are the greatest babysitters—and friends—imaginable, and nothing would make me prouder than to have you be the first people in the world to wear Goldie Chic Originals scarves!"

Later, as JoJo was preparing to take the stage to perform a few songs to wrap up the party, her friends gathered to look at each other's scarves. Not surprisingly, the scarves were like beautiful works of art, and Goldie had chosen colors and patterns that perfectly suited each of their styles.

"I'm going to wear mine when I give my book report tomorrow," Grace said, holding her silky yellow ombré scarf up for everyone to see.

"I'm going to wear mine basically every day of my life," Miley sighed. She had already tied her pastel polka-dotted scarf around her neck.

"I wish I had something to give you guys to say thank you," Kyra said as she hugged her gift bag close to her chest. "I never could have pulled everything off without your help."

"That's what friends are for," Jacob said.

"And next time you won't wait 'til the last moment to ask for help, right?" Grace added, linking her arm through Kyra's.

"Believe me, I learned my lesson!" Kyra exclaimed.

Just then, the sound engineer walked over.

"JoJo, are you ready?" he asked.

"Let's make this happen!" JoJo cheered, handing her gift bag to Miley for safekeeping.

As JoJo headed onto the stage, she thought about how happy she was that everything had turned out so perfectly. And her special rhinestone-studded scarf, which she would treasure forever, was the icing on the tiara cake!

MORE BOOKS AVAILABLE . . .

. . . BY JOJO SIWA!